Mary Jean Hendrick

If Anything Goes Wrong at the Zoo Ever

illustrated by Jane Dyer

Voyager Books
Harcourt Brace & Company

San Diego   New York   London

First Voyager Books edition 1996
Voyager Books is a registered trademark of Harcourt Brace & Company.

Library of Congress Cataloging-in-Publication Data
Hendrick, Mary Jean.
If anything ever goes wrong at the zoo/Mary Jean Hendrick;
illustrated by Jane Dyer.—1st ed.
p.   cm.
"Voyager Books."
Summary: After a young girl tells the zookeepers to send the animals to her
house should anything go wrong at the zoo, a series of zoo emergencies
results in some unusual houseguests for the girl and her family.
ISBN 0-15-238007-8   ISBN 0-15-201009-2 pb
[1. Zoo animals—Fiction.] I. Dyer, Jane, ill. II. Title.
PZ7.H385641If   1993   [E]—dc20   91-25566

H G F E D

Printed in Singapore

The illustrations in this book were painted in Winsor & Newton
watercolors on Waterford 140-lb. hot-press paper.
The display type and text type were set in Perpetua
by Harcourt Brace & Company Photocomposition Center, San Diego, California.
Color separations by Bright Arts, Ltd., Singapore
Printed and bound by Tien Wah Press, Singapore
This book was printed on Arctic matte paper.
Production supervision by Warren Wallerstein and Diana Ford
Designed by Camilla Filancia

For Seth, Leslie, and all
the other children who read,
enjoyed, and asked for more.
And for Lois and Dotty.
—M. J. H.

For Larry, Sandy,
Matthew, and Chris.
—J. D.

Leslie and her mother went to the zoo every Saturday.

One Saturday Leslie talked to Seth, the zebra keeper.

"Could I have a zebra?" asked Leslie.

"Oh, no," said Seth. "Zebras need to stay at the zoo in their nice fenced yard."

"Well," said Leslie. "I have a nice fenced yard. If anything ever goes wrong at the zoo, you can send the zebras to my house. It's the one on the top of the hill."

"Thank you," said Seth. "I'll remember that."

The next Saturday, Leslie talked to David, the monkey keeper.

"Could I have a monkey?" asked Leslie.

"Oh, no," said David. "Monkeys need lots of room to exercise. They need things to swing on, and they like lots of bananas. Monkeys must stay at the zoo."

"Well," said Leslie, "I have a very large swing set. And we always have lots of bananas. If anything ever goes wrong at the zoo, you can send the monkeys to my house."

"Thank you," said David. "I'll remember that."

The next Saturday, Leslie watched the elephants.

"Could I have an elephant?" Leslie asked Joanna, the elephant keeper.

"Oh, no," she replied. "You need a very large place to put an elephant."

"Well," said Leslie, "I have a very large garage. If anything ever goes wrong at the zoo, you can send the elephants to my house."

"Thank you," said Joanna. "I'll remember that."

Every Saturday Leslie invited another animal to her house, but none of them ever came.

Then one Saturday it was too wet to go to the zoo. It had rained all day Friday. On Saturday it was still raining. Leslie looked out the window. The street looked like a river.

"Mom," asked Leslie. "Do houses float?"

"No, houses don't float," Leslie's mother answered. "But our house is on the top of the hill. I don't think the water will come up this far."

"Mom," asked Leslie, "is the zoo on a hill?"

"No," said her mother, "but I'm sure someone knows what to do if anything ever goes wrong at the zoo."

"Oh, yes." Leslie nodded. "They know just what to do."

It was still raining when Leslie and her mother went to bed. They had not been in bed long when the doorbell rang.

"Hurry, hurry," a voice called. "Something's gone wrong at the zoo."

Leslie's mother opened the door. There was Seth, the zebra keeper, with five zebras.

"The zoo is flooding!" Seth said. "Is this Leslie's house?"

"Why, yes, it is," said Leslie's mother.

"Oh, thank you," said Seth, and he put the zebras in the backyard.

Then a truck pulled into the driveway.

Joanna, the elephant keeper, rolled down the window and called through the rain, "Is this Leslie's house?"

"Why, yes, it is," Leslie's mother called back.

"How can we ever thank you?" Joanna shouted, and she put three elephants in the garage.

When Leslie and her mother went back into the house, David was at the back door. "This is the house where Leslie lives, isn't it?" he asked.

"Why, yes, it is," replied Leslie's mother.

"Thought so—I saw the zebras," David said. "I put the monkeys on the swing set. Thank you!" He smiled, and then he was gone.

All night long the animals came. There was a lion in the closet. An alligator splashed in the tub.

Goats nibbled on the bed pillows, and ostriches raced down the hall.
"They're very noisy houseguests," said Leslie's mother.
"Even worse than Mary Ellen," agreed Leslie.

In the morning, the rain had stopped. The zookeepers came to take the animals back to the zoo.

Seth was the last to arrive. He came to the front door.

"Thank you, Leslie," he said. "I'm glad I remembered that if anything ever went wrong at the zoo, we could bring the animals to your house." He and the zebras followed the monkeys down the hill.

"Leslie, did you invite all those animals to our house?"

"Well, yes, Mom," admitted Leslie, "but only if anything ever went wrong at the zoo."

"Well," said her mother, "The next time you invite friends home, would you check with me first? We wouldn't want anything to ever go wrong at our house."

And Leslie promised.